LifeRich Publishing is a registered trademark of The Reader's Digest Association, Inc.

LifeRich Publishing books may be ordered through booksellers or by contacting:

LifeRich Publishing
1663 Liberty Drive
Bloomington, IN 47403
www.liferichpublishing.com
844-686-9607

ISBN: 978-1-4897-3849-3 (sc)
ISBN: 978-1-4897-3848-6 (e)

Library of Congress Control Number: 2021919585

Print information available on the last page.

LifeRich Publishing rev. date:  10/13/2021

# Big Cheeks

## Desert Adventure

Written and Illustrated by Laura Planck

**These books were created to show the joy of helping those in need.**

Big Cheeks from Squirrely Beach is invited by his cousin Zippy, the rock squirrel to come have some fun in the desert. They start their adventure with a dirt bike ride and find a baby javelina lost from her family. They come to her rescue. It won't be an easy job reuniting them because there are lots of areas to explore, with plenty of critters along the way. They have to watch out for the sneaky snakes too.

· · · · · · · · · · · · · · · · · · · · · · · · · · · · · · · · · · · · · · ·

## Author & Illustrator, Laura Planck

Laura has been blessed as a graphic designer for 40 years. When she retired she wanted to illustrate and write children's books. It has been a dream of hers since High School.

She and her family lived in sunny southern California. They frequently took their dog Angel to the dog beach where her stories take place. The ground squirrel families play around the rocks and enjoy being feed by the visitors.

Laura's experience comes from a fulfilled life of being a Christian mom, wife, and business owner. She desires to )continue to use her talents for God. She wants her books to put a big smile on children's faces and give them good wholesome stories to read.

# Big Cheek's
## Desert Adventure

Happy Helping
stories for kids

Other stories in this series written and illustrated by Laura Planck
Big Cheeks at Squirrely Beach & Corgi Day at Squirrely Beach

It was a beautiful sunny day at Squirrely Beach. Big Cheeks was sitting on his favorite rock. He saw Pelican Pete flying over with a message.

Big Cheeks started reading the message that Pelican Pete brought to him.

Dear Big Cheeks,
This is your cousin Zippy in Arizona. How's it going at that silly sandy beach? You should come to see me and we will have lots of fun in the desert. My address is 1234 Rocky Rock, AZ.
Love,

Zippy

Zippy is a strong little rock squirrel that lives in the high desert. His home is on the rocks. He loves to mountain bike and eat ice cream when it's hot.

Big Cheeks hopped on a truck full of oranges going to Arizona. He asked the driver to please drop him off at 1234 Rocky Rock.

Big Cheeks and Zippy were so happy to see each other again. They started planning all the fun things to do. "Let's go biking on the trails!" said Zippy. "Yahoo hoosker doo!" said Big Cheeks.

Nearby, a family of javelina was eating and rubbing their hinnies on the rocks. Suddenly, they heard loud laughter coming from the trail. It scared them, so they ran away and accidentally left the baby behind.

At the bottom of the trail stood a crying baby javelina. "What's the matter asked Big Cheeks?" "My name is Honey. I'm lost and can't find my family."

Big Cheeks told Honey, "Don't worry we will help you find them." Zippy was not happy. He wanted to have fun and did not like those stinky critters with scary teeth.

Big Cheeks, Honey, and Zippy started their desert adventure. "I will go, but watch out for the sneaky snakes. They like ice cream," said Zippy. "God will keep us safe," said Big Cheeks

Zippy asked Tina the tarantula if she had seen any javelinas? "Nope. They didn't step on me today."

Zippy asked Darla the deer if she had seen any of Honey's family eating around the Cafe'?

Darla only saw the big, hungry, people but she did see Honey's family by the lake.

They went down to the water to look around. Ducks were swimming and a Bald Eagle flew by with a fish. Then Big Cheeks saw a javelina with a stick floating on a big board.

"Wow! Is that your mama or papa Honey?"
"No just one of my neighbors trying to paddleboard."

They went down to the valley. "Howdy Wolfey!" said Zippy "We're looking for a family of javelinas. Did any run through here today?"

The next day was really cold but they had to keep looking. Jack the rabbit said he didn't see any javelinas playing in the snow.

Hooty the Owl was in a nearby tree and heard the question. "I know where Honey's family is. Follow me!"

The snow was starting to melt and go away. Everyone was beginning to get very excited about finding Honey's family.

Hooty was so happy to help and wanted to get there fast as possible but he had to slow down a little so they could keep up.

Hooty flew to the bridge. He told them this is where the javelinas like to go at the end of the day. Honey and her family were so happy, you could hear them snorting really loud with joy.

Zippy was so happy, he gave his
ice cream to the sneaky snake.
Big Cheeks said "Thank you God for bringing
us all safely back together."

CPSIA information can be obtained
at www.ICGtesting.com
Printed in the USA
BVHW021414261021
619925BV00019B/1011

9 781489 738493